I'll Hug You More

L.D.

For my nieces and nephews, especially CJ who
promises to be an honorable "Ambassador of Hugs"

M.I.

To Jamie, my panda child—I love you!

Published by Sourcebooks Jabberwocky, an imprint of Sourcebooks, Inc.
P.O. Box 4410, Naperville, Illinois 60567-4410
(630) 961-3900
Fax: (630) 961-2168
www.jabberwockykids.com

Library of Congress Cataloging-in-Publication Data

Names: Duksta, Laura, author.
Title: I'll hug you more / Laura Duksta.
Other titles: I will hug you more
Description: Naperville, IL : Sourcebooks Jabberwocky, [2017] | Summary: "Rise and shine, it's time to start our day, with an "I Love you" and a big hug to get you on your way. Hugs can say a lot of things like "hello," "thank you," and "i'm sorry." But underneath it all, every hug says "I love you." Explore the depths of the special bond between parent and child through the universal gesture of a hug"-- Provided by publisher.Identifiers: LCCN 2016000713 | (13 : alk. paper)
Subjects: | CYAC: Stories in rhyme. | Hugging--Fiction. | Love--Fiction. |
Parent and child--Fiction.
Classification: LCC PZ8.3.D885 Il 2017 | DDC [E]--dc23 LC record available at https://lccn.loc.gov/2016000713

Source of Production: Leo Paper, Heshan City, Guangdong Province, China
Date of Production: October 2016
Run Number: 5007503

Printed and bound in China.
LEO 10 9 8 7 6 5 4 3 2 1

Written by Laura Duksta   Illustrated by Melissa Iwai

Rise and shine. It's time to start our day
with an "I love you" and a big hug—
we're off and on our way!

I'll hug you to say thank-you
for getting my breakfast ready.

I'll hug you and snuggle with you
and my favorite teddy.

I'll hug you around your leg
because that's as high as I can reach.

I'll hug you after a yummy snack,
maybe a giant peach.

I'll hug you when I get home from school and share about my day.

I'll hug you after we sit and color
on the floor and play.

I'll hug you
when I'm done with my bath
and have my pajamas on.

I'll hug you when it's time for bed,
with a stretch and a great big yawn.

Now that our day is done
and it's time to say good night,
I tell you, "I love you more,"
before you turn out my light.

When the new day starts again,
this I know for sure,
I won't just hug you
one more time...

Tomorrow, I'll hug you more!

I'll hug you more and more and more and more!

I'll hug you more and more and more!

And when the new day starts again,
I won't just hug you one more time...
Tomorrow, I'll hug you more!

I'll softly whisper, "I love you,"
and hear you say, "I love you more."

When our day is done
and it's time to say good night,
I'll wrap my arms around you
and hug you real tight.

I'll hug you on a stormy night
and keep you safe with me.

I'll hug you as we swing together
in the old oak tree.

I'll hug you as we gaze
at the shining stars
and together make a wish.

I'll hug you and dry you off
when you're done
swimming like a fish.

I'll hug you after we come in
from playing with friends outside.

I'll hug you when I buckle you up
before we go for a ride.

I'll hug you as we read a book
up on our comfy chair.

I'll hug you and tickle your toes
and spin you in the air.

Rise and shine. It's time to start our day
with an "I love you" and a big hug
to get you on your way…

§ sourcebooks
jabberwocky

Written by Laura Duksta
Illustrated by Melissa Iwai

I'll Hug You More